Punj

Other Stories

Punjab Singh
and
Other Stories

Kartar Singh Duggal

Rupa & Co

Published 2002 by
Rupa & Co
7/16, Ansari Road, Daryaganj,
New Delhi 110 002

Sales Centres:

Allahabad Bangalore Chandigarh Chennai
Dehradun Hyderabad Jaipur Kathmandu
Kolkata Ludhiana Mumbai Pune

These stories are translations
from the original Punjabi

ISBN 81-7167-918-8

Typeset 12 pts. Aldine by
Nikita Overseas Pvt Ltd,
1410 Chiranjiv Tower,
43 Nehru Place
New Delhi 110 019

Printed in India by
Saurabh Print-O-Pack
A 15-16 Sector IV
Noida (UP)

Contents

The Making of a Militant

Mangu was the first-born. His father Marhu was a so-called low-caste *chamar*. But they had given up the calling long ago. His father's father had taken to farming. They worked as farm labourers in the employ of the *biswedar*. No longer did they pursue their caste profession of treating the hides of dead cattle.

As tenants, they had to work hard. They ploughed the land, sowed seed, tended and reaped the crop when ripe, gathered the harvest and filled the landlord's bins before they engaged themselves with the next crop. The endless cycle from *kharif* to *rabi* and from *rabi* to *kharif* continued from year to year.

Marhu Ram did it. So did Marhu Ram's father. And now Mangu had to join his father like a beast of burden. They had to toil very hard to be elevated from the incarnation of a *chamar* to that of tenant. They were particularly happy that the landlord was *sarkar*. So did the other farm-hands.

That they were *chamars* by caste, Marhu Ram had forgotten long ago. He would never mention it. But he was amazed to notice that his son Mangu seemed to take pride in being born a *chamar*. The other day when the census enumerators visited them, while his father was evasive, Mangu told them in so many words: "We are *chamars* by caste though we have taken to farming. My father's father and his father were low-caste *chamars*." Marhu Ram heard it and felt small. They were *chamars* all right, but where was the need to publicise it? The calling of a farm hand was tidy and he was happy to belong to it.

Marhu Ram at times imagined that the way the Government promised to better the lot of the scheduled castes and scheduled tribes, he wouldn't be surprised if his son rose to be a regular farmer one day. They had already turned tenants from tanners. They had scaled some stairs; they might scale a few more. The Government was committed to undo unevenness in society. The land must go to the landless, who cultivated it. Jobs were being reserved for the backward classes. New tenements were being provided to them at subsidised prices. And many more amenities waited to be made public.

Marhu Ram had his son go to school and pass matriculation. The boy was intelligent. Everyone believed that he was going to be a big officer.

But as ill-luck would have it, Marhu Ram's son would have none of it. He started speaking quite a different language: That this government is good for nothing; the rich are becoming richer and the poor are getting poorer. That we must fight for our rights; this government must go, come what may. Marhu Ram's hopes were dashed to pieces.

He tried to explain to his son: It seems someone has misled you. The government has decided to allot land to the cultivators. At places *pattas* have already been granted to landless labourers.

'Bunkum!' Mangu heard his father and flared up: All this is untrue. Deeds are drawn up but they remain on paper all along; nobody gets land, nobody gives land. Those who have gone to the court, their legs have been broken. Their houses are set on the fire and they are driven away. Mangu would then enumerate the names of villages in UP and Bihar, Madhya Pradesh and Orissa where such atrocities had been perpetrated.

Marhu Ram's eyes opened when what his son Mangu told him, happened in their own neighbourhood. In the village next to theirs, when the tenants agitated for their rights, the landlord employed *goondas* to teach them a lesson. Their houses were burnt. Their women were raped. Their menfolk were massacred.

Marhu Ram advised his son not to take notice of such happenings. "He who wields power must have his way," he said, "The tenants in their neighbourhood must have misbehaved so the landlord had to take such a drastic measure." Their own *biswedar* would never do such a thing. From poor *chamars* whose lot it was to take charge of the dead cattle and tan their hides, they had become respectable tenants. What more did they want? If they had anything better to gain in their lot, they would be blessed with it in due course. "Even as it is, the land in a way belongs to us." Marhu Ram maintained, "We plough, we sow and we harvest the crop. The farm livestock is at our disposal. So much so that the *biswedar's* personal horse is more attached to me than to the master."

Mangu listened to his father and pitied him for his deceiving himself with such false notions. The father and son were always at logger-heads.

Rather than taking up a *sarkari* job and aspiring to be a big officer in due course, Marhu Ram's son talked of changing the existing set-up. "When peasants and workers join hands," he said, "the fabric of the prevalent system would snap. We are more in number and the word of the majority must prevail."

Marhu Ram heard it and felt distressed. He, however, had one consolation. His son had nothing to do with the militants. Several young men in the village had gone over to them. They would flaunt their weapons and carry three-foot long swords in broad day-light. Mangu was not known to possess even a blunt knife.

Marhu persuaded his son to visit the temple both times, morning and evening. He would narrate to him stories from the Ramayana and the Mahabharata. Mangu did whatever his father wished him to do. He tried not to annoy him unnecessarily. It was a different matter that on certain issues they did not see eye to eye with each other.

Then someone advised Marhu to get his son married. With a wife to look after he would be more responsible, more steady. Marhu Ram talked to his son. He resisted the proposal for a while, but when his father insisted, he gave in. Essentially an obedient child, if he could help it, he would not displease his father.

The moment he gave his consent, there were ever so many offers for Mangu. A handsome young man who had studied upto matriculation, Mangu had no dearth of matches. He had only to decide whom he would like to have for his bride. There were scores of eligible girls in their community.

Mangu's wedding was a memorable event.

Liquor flowed like water both at the bridegroom's and at the bride's house. The marriage party danced *bhangra* and played *sammi* like mad. It was the same when they brought home the bride. Mangu's father showered coins on the bride as her *doli* entered their village. His mother performed ever so many ceremonies on the auspicious occasion of the bride's stepping on their threshold.

And she was no ordinary bride. Her name was Saleti, the maiden name of Heer. A glimpse of her and everyone around was enamoured of her. She was more beautiful than anyone they had known. An image of comeliness. It was said that she sang and danced like a fairy from heaven. Mangu's mother's joy knew no bounds. The neighbours who came to see her were overwhelmed with her figure and charm. She was going to be the pride of the village. Everyone congratulated Mangu's mother and father on this alliance.

Mangu, the bridegroom, was in the meanwhile entertaining his friends. Some of them could not accompany the marriage party. They wished to celebrate for having brought such a prize bride to their village in marriage. They drank till late in the night.

Marhu Ram was happy that he had weaned away his son from undesirable company. He would now have nothing to do with the spoilt youth of the village. They roamed about without let or hindrance. They carried all sorts of weapons on their person. Then they would get into the police net. Some would be shot in the so-called encounters. Others would be taken into custody to rot in jails indefinitely.

It was past midnight when Mangu's party concluded. Inebriated, more at the thought of consorting with a charming bride than the liquor he had consumed, Mangu walked to his room, his steps faltering. As he entered the room, he was amazed to find it empty, the bride was nowhere to be seen.

Where could she have gone? Bewildered, Mangu came out of his room. He was looking around for her when his mother noticing her son's discomfiture told him, "*Beta*, the bride has gone to the *biswedar*. She will be back soon."

"But why? What has she to do with the *biswedar* at this hour of night?"

"*Beta*..." and the rest of it was stuck in his mother's throat.

In the meanwhile his father came out of his room and explained: "The bride has to spend the first night at *biswedar's*."

Mangu heard it and he collapsed where he was.

"This is his privilege," Mangu's father tried to argue, "One has to follow the tradition. Your mother, too, did it in her time."

"Then, it is true what people say!" Mangu muttered to himself. He felt as if a bomb had burst. There was thick smoke that suffocated him. The earth had given way and he was sinking in it. There were walls of darkness all around him.

The next moment Mangu collected himself. He walked to the stable and dug a corner and pulling out a buried weapon, left his house.

Not many days had passed when news came that the Government had announced an award of one lakh rupees for anyone who would help arrest Mangu Ram, son of Marhu Ram of village Talwandi biswedar.

Come Back, My Master

Neeli was white, as white as a pat of butter washed in milk. And she was strong and handsome.

"A healthy and handsome cow's milk is also wholesome," my wife would often say. No wonder she had chosen Neeli from the milkman's large herd.

Every morning Neeli was led to our house. Standing under the *pipal* tree, she filled the jar with warm, fragrant milk. And then she was led away.

Neeli came to our house, the milkman following her, with her feed in a wooden trough on his head. He placed the trough before her and started caressing her skin with his large knuckled hands. Then, after a final pat, he sat beside her, holding the jar between his knees. Silvery streaks of milk made joyous music as they dropped into the brass jar.

While the milkman was thus engaged, Neeli continued browsing chaff mixed with bran, oil-cake and cottonseed in the trough. A rich, ample feed for Neeli was one of the stipulations laid down by my wife. And she often checked on the contents of the trough. "If the animal is fed well, you will have better milk and more butter," said my wife.

Neeli came every morning. From the eagerness with which she turned the corner to enter the gate, it appeared as if she was every inch impatient. Was it for the spicy food, I wondered, or was it for the pleasure of being relieved of her milky burden?

Thus, Neeli visited our house every day. She came early in the morning when we were either asleep, or had just awakened. And soon she was gone, escorted by the milkman.

Several months passed. And then we heard one day that Neeli had refused to give milk. When after many weeks she returned, she was followed by a milk-white, tender calf, with timid, innocent eyes.

Our consumption of milk seemed to be conditioned by Neeli's morning yield. We bought the whole lot, and the milkman strained out the last drop to augment the supply. My wife felt, he was not leaving any milk for the young calf to suck. She often warned him that he was starving the young one. But he paid little heed to it.

The milkman now started skimping on Neeli's feed also. With a suckling calf to help, he thought she needed no further bait to "bring" the milk. My wife repeatedly complained that the milk was no longer of the same quality as before. Her other regret was that the calf was being reduced to a pack of bones, starved as it was.

"She always holds back some milk for the calf," was the milkman's reply to my wife every time. To prove his point, he would show her the calf eagerly tugging at its mother's dry teats.

My wife's worst fears turned out to be true. Starved and famished, one day the calf died.

The milkman wore a long face as he came

to our house the next morning. Neeli was not with him. He sorrowfully said that the calf had died, that Neeli had not eaten at all since the previous evening. We would have to arrange milk from elsewhere for the day.

My wife was distressed. She could not pardon the milkman. He had deliberately killed the calf. Neeli might refuse to give milk altogether.

"He has been such an ass!" said my wife, after the milkman had gone. There was more pity in her words than anger. "Trying to save a few ounces of milk each day, he has lost the calf who, in its time, would have grown into a splendid cow."

Next morning Neeli came. She quietly stopped at the gate. Normally, when she found the gate barred, she would attempt to force it open with her horns. But not today. She stood at the gate, forlorn and desolate.

The milkman came and opened the gate. Neeli followed him with slow, unwilling steps.

I watched the scene from the verandah. Beside me stood my wife, holding to her breast our little daughter.

The milkman placed the trough under the

pipal tree, and started raking up the contents to tempt Neeli with the piquant smell of oil-cake. But Neeli would not go. The smell of oil-cake seemed to tempt her no longer. When at last she reached her usual spot, she completely ignored the trough. The milkman again put his hand into the trough, and, picking a handful of gram, he offered it to her on his open palm.

Neeli advanced a step towards the milkman and then paused. She seemed again to go forward, but suddenly turned her face away. The trough containing gram, cottonseed and oil-cake did not interest her.

The milkman started stroking Neeli's forehead. He fondly hummed to her. Then he sat by the trough and shook it once again. The smell of oil-cake came up. Neeli was startled out of her dreamy languor. She was automatically drawn towards the trough and she dipped her snout into it. But she did not eat. After a while, she withdrew and slowly turned her back on the trough. She could not eat today.

The milkman cast one bewildered glance towards us, raised the trough to his head and went out of the gate, followed by Neeli.

"For the sake of a little milk he has killed the poor creature," mumbled my wife gloomily, as she went inside the house to ask the servant to fetch milk from the dairy.

I could still see the milkman going down the road with the trough on his head. Behind him went Neeli, slowly and heavily, as if groping in darkness.

"From the dairy, bring a little cow-dung also. Tomorrow is the sacred day of *Sankrant,* and we will need it to line the oven." I heard my wife give further instructions to the servant as Neeli slowly faded away into the distance.

Next morning I heard the gate open earlier than usual. It was the milkman and Neeli. I went out onto the verandah and saw Neeli raise her nostrils towards the trough on the milkman's head.

"The milkman has won the battle," I said to myself.

I was not wrong. As the milkman placed the trough under the *pipal* tree, Neeli stepped forward and began feeding. She had gone without feed for two days.

Seeing her eat, the milkman sat beside her with the jar. Neeli stepped aside.

The milkman turned his face to glance at the trough. Neeli was eating with her head lowered into it. Reassured, he moved up closer. But Neeli stepped further aside.

The milkman stood up in dismay.

With her face buried in the trough, Neeli was slowly munching her food. She had not eaten for the past two days.

The milkman waited for a few minutes. He then gently scratched Neeli's skin with his finger-tips, gave her a pat on the back and sat down once again to draw milk. Neeli was busy munching, but no sooner did he touch her teat than she suddenly jerked away.

The milkman made another attempt after a while. Neeli lunged aside, this time lashing out angrily with one of her legs.

The milkman was in a rage. He looked fiercely at Neeli. She was chewing away quietly, as though nothing had happened.

Snatching the trough, he raised it to his head and walked away angrily. Neeli stood stupefied for a second and then turned to look in the direction in which he had gone. When he reached the gate, Neeli lowed. The milkman did not stop.

For a long time Neeli kept looking in the same direction, her eyes dolefully riveted on the gate. She waited for the milkman, uttering mournful lows as if she were saying, "Come back, my master! Come back, my master! Why don't you understand that I have lost my child—the flesh of my flesh, the blood of my blood? Come back, my master! And where do I say that I would deny you my milk? I shall give you the milk. A day or two and I will forget my beloved child. And then you can milk me. Placing the bait before me, you may milk me dry. Come back, my master! Don't starve me. I am hungry. Come back, my master!"

Standing under the *pipal* tree, Neeli kept steadily looking towards the gate.

The milkman did not return.

Punjab Singh

Chando was sick of it. The people around were constantly insinuating. They indulged in all sorts of irresponsible gossip. Good for nothing, the whole lot of them. Her husband Punjoo was a gem of a man. He got up early in the morning to say his prayers. He never skipped the prescribed recital before going to bed. At times even…

And a smile played on Chando's lips. Does anyone recite the scriptures at midnight? She would be lying in rapturous delight under the cool shadow of the late night stars, when she would hear her husband say his prayers just after returning to his bed. Before he finished the recital, Chando would be fast asleep. They had been married barely for a year. The youthful days when the moment you get into bed, you drop into the lap of sleep.

But where does he go these days? Chando wondered. Of late, he had started staying away from home without telling her about it. He would leave early in the morning and return late in the evening. At times she had to wait for him the night through. Does one ever leave a young bride all alone like that? More, in these days of unrest all around. What atrocities were committed! People were killed like flies. Whether it was an extremist's bullet or that of a security man, it killed a human being. The victims were, more often than not, innocent people. Someone's husband, someone's son, someone's brother! Blood-splattered streets, wailing women, terror stalking the countryside!

Sitting alone in her courtyard, Chando would, at times, feel miserable. She longed for company. Her husband, Punjoo, was the only son of his parents who had died long ago. The only company she had was that of the neighbours. They, too, had changed of late. What nonsense they talked! 'Punjoo has got into bad company!' every time any one of them opened his mouth, he would say.

What bad company?

Chando didn't see anything wrong with her man. He had hardly finished his studies, when his people got him married. A university graduate, how well he talked in English! He would always read English newspapers. The only change Chando found in him was that he did not appear to give due attention to farming these days. But that could be because of cheap labour that was made available. Trainloads of farm hands came from the neighbouring states and took over the agricultural operations from the farmers, leaving them free to indulge in drinking and merrymaking.

Her husband, however, did no such thing. He had his own tractor. He would drive it to his fields and attend to ploughing and sowing, reaping and garnering with his own hands. There was no scarcity of canal water. He did engage labourers to assist him. But no more. He was always fair to them. He never deprived anyone of his due. He had the utmost regard for the fair name of his father. His father had been the elder of the village. No one had ever dared to defy him.

Lost in thought, Chando entered the interiormost room of the house that she had neither swept nor dusted for the past several months. Her entire dower was stored in this room. The big trunk, her sewing machine, the multi-coloured settee, the peacock-feather fan that her mother had made with her own hands and what not. Chando had kept apart the multi- coloured settee and the peacock-feather fan to be taken out only when she became the mother of a son. Sitting on the settee by the baby's cot, she would fan him with the peacock feathers. As she would do so, she would sing a lullaby:

It's a mother's lullaby
Whose breasts overflow with milk

The mention of milk reminded Chando that their cow had gone dry. She lowed and called again and again last night. Had her husband been at home, she would have sent the cow, the first thing, to the village stud. They had acquired an excellent bull last month. The thought gave Chando a queer sensation in her womb. Her period too was overdue. They had been married for a year.

How much longer would God have her wait? Her friend Chinto was already the mother of a child. They were married the same full moon fortnight last spring.

Sunk in thought, Chando went deeper in the innermost room. And what is it that she saw? A virtual arsenal of arms and ammunition; guns and hand grenades, carbines and cartridges. Chando was thunderstruck. She missed a heartbeat. She started perspiring all over. Who had dumped all those weapons in her house? Why had she not been told about it? And then it seemed a bomb burst in her bosom. The neighbours were evidently not wrong. It was her husband. It was his doing. Indeed, he was keeping bad company. That explained why he remained to himself. God knows what books he read. The ship of her life had been wrecked.

Suddenly she experienced an uncanny fright in the semi-dark room. She withdrew herself hurriedly and came to the living room. She had a queer sinking sensation. The next moment she collapsed on her bed.

Chando remembered that not many days ago a number of passengers had been pulled out of a bus and mercilessly massacred. It must be the doing of her husband! The outrage had been perpetrated outside their village on the highway. Punjoo was absent from home that night. When he returned the next morning, she told him about the dastardly happening. She was amazed to notice that her husband hardly reacted to the tragic incident, as if he had not heard about it. Far from condemning it, he had asked for a glass of sherbet; he was terribly thirsty, he said. Her friend Devki's brother had been shot in the next village. Maybe that too was her husband Punjoo's doing. Then Bhago, Tapo, Guddi, Radha, Sundri, Sukanya– one after the other a number of her friends had been widowed. They were Chando's playmates. Blood-splattered streets, wailing women, terror stalking the countryside, lost in these thoughts Chando went to sleep.

She remained asleep for quite some time. When she opened her eyes, she found her husband back home. He had already taken his bath and was reading scriptures from the holy book. Chando got up and went to the kitchen. She knew, as soon as he finished his prayers he would ask for his meal.

Chando told herself that she would talk to him about the arms and ammunition after he had eaten. She would like to know why he had started staying away from home these days. People talked all sorts of nonsense. He must have some regard for his father's fair name. They had just started their life as husband and wife. Chando had a bosom full of dreams to fulfil.

She was still busy in the kitchen when Punjoo finished his prayers. He went out in the courtyard and climbed his tractor. He said, "In a hurry yesterday I left it in the middle of the compound, let me drive it to a side."

As he reversed the tractor, one of the many chicks of their hen got crushed under the rear wheel. The hen started clucking vociferously along with her brood, going round and round.

Punjoo heard it and stopped the tractor at once. He jumped down instantaneously. Yes, one of the chicks had been crushed under the wheel of the tractor. He picked up the chick in both hands and tears gushed out of his eyes. The hen along with the rest of the chicks continued to fume and flutter.

Punjoo stood in the compound looking at

the crushed chick for long. His hands were smeared with blood. The murderer! His face went pale as if he had committed a heinous crime.

Chando saw it all. Taking him by the arm, she pulled him to the verandah. She took the crushed chick from him and kept it aside. She washed his hands with soap. She then went to the kitchen and brought his meal. He had not eaten since morning. Seeing the meal, Punjoo's eyes filled again. He pushed the tray aside. He could not eat.

Chando tried to explain to him. Another week or so and they would have slaughtered, dressed and cooked the fowl for the table. Punjoo would hear no such argument. He was crestfallen, in deep agony. There was a pall of grief around him. If the man in the house doesn't eat, how can anyone else do so?

The chick crushed under the tractor lay on the floor. Every time Punjoo saw it his eyes would be filled with tears. Chando was at a loss to know how to make him forget it when a jeep loaded with armed policemen came and stopped outside their house. The next moment they landed in their courtyard. They were being led by an inspector. 'Sir, he is Punjoo, Punjab Singh." someone among them pointed to Chando's husband. As he said it, the armed securitymen swooped upon the hard-core militant and handcuffed him.

The Masters

Back in our village there were a few zamindar families. We called them 'masters'. Their cattle could graze in any field. They could ask anyone in the street to do anything for them. And it was done. Their evil eye could fall on any young girl and none dared protest. It was left to the girls to take care of themselves. And the young girls of the village would cover their faces with heavy veils when they came out into the street. Even the British rulers had given the zamindars special privileges. The tax they collected at the cattle fair every Tuesday would go into their pockets and not deposited in the Government

Treasury. Their clothes were white as the cream of milk they drank. Keeping them white was the back-breaking chore for the village washerman. Anything the zamindars wanted was given to them as a gift, even if they just hinted at it. Not only that, even if one of their dogs passed by in the street, people would stand up in respect! Their joy was the joy of the village and if they were unhappy, so was the entire village. For were they not the masters, the privileged ones?

Then India became free. With independence the country was divided. No one can forget the days of freedom and the turbulence partition brought in its wake. Our zamindars, however, protected the Hindu and Sikh neighbours in their large houses. But when that was no longer possible, we had to leave. They put us in trucks and left us on the border. Their eyes were full of tears. We wept for them, our protectors, the masters!

The house that we were allotted in Amritsar was a little distance away from the town. There were only a few houses in the neighbourhood. Next door to us lived a one-time prince of a neighbouring state. He had bought six houses in the town. In one of them, he lived and the others he rented out to those like us. It was not long that the neighbours' children began mixing with our children. We also started having visits of the lady of the house next door which my wife reciprocated. And very soon after, we were on constant visiting terms with each other, borrowing things and such other neighbourly give-and-take. We got used to calling our neighbours Raja Saheb and Rani Saheba as befitted their old status. Often the Rani Saheba would sit with my wife and talk about the past glorious days till late in the night. The stories she told seemed exotic and like fairy tales: their life in the big palace, their princely grandeur and the secrets of their boudoir. Wistfully the Rani would recount the old tales while my commoner wife would listen to them with rapt attention. Was it not strange indeed that a lowly Government servant was living as the next-door neighbour of a royal prince and a princess? If the Rani Saheba ever got angry with the Raja Saheb, she would come to our house and assuage her anger after having told us about it. Her servants were a big problem;

one was a thief, the other talked too much, the third had no manners, the fourth was intolerably lazy. All except an old maid servant who had been with them during the good old days: she alone was there to remind them of their lost grandeur.

One day as I was strolling about in our garden, I heard the maidservant talking to our neighbour's little son. She was beseeching him to come and eat his dinner. Every now and then she would call him, 'Little Master, My Master.' Over and over again. And when I heard her, my mind went back to our village and the zamindar, whom we used to call 'The Master,' whose cattle could graze in any field, who could ask anyone in the street to do anything for him. And it was done, whose evil eye could fall on any young girl and none dared protest. Those whom the British rulers had given special privileges.

Not many years later, we were transferred to a city much bigger than Amritsar, leaving behind our royal neighbours, the prince and the princess. A quiet town, we cherished its peace when suddenly it became a beehive of activity. The Municipal elections were in the offing. Every evening there would be a procession, big or small, and of different kinds, with their separate flags flying and their slogan-mongering. And at nights there would be speeches and songs. And musical recitals. Amplified by so many loud-speakers, we could hear them sitting on our verandah. And we could see them all as they passed through our street. One group went on motor cars. The symbol of that particular party was a motor car. Another party whose symbol was a horse-cart, came in horse-carts. Yet another in bullock-carts; each party proclaiming its identity and its special eligibility. Each one louder than the other. And after the grown-ups came the little children, shouting now for one party, then for another.

A few days went by. Then one day municipal employees came to distribute identity cards for the elections. I had one vote. My wife also had one. The elections were after three days; the polling booth was at a distance of three hundred yards in the primary school.

At last the day of the elections arrived. We got up in the morning with the same thought in mind.

'Whom are we going to vote for?' I asked.

'Nobody has come and asked us.' My wife answered.

That was true. No party had approached us.

'At any rate,' she went on, 'if anyone comes asking for our vote, I will tell him that only the one who gets this drain in front of our house covered will get our vote.'

True, I agreed. That drain stank to high heaven.

'And not only the drain,' she went on, 'how about that garbage on the play-ground opposite? And the street that is never swept? And the refuse that piles up and gets stinking wet every time it rains and breeds deadly germs? The municipality should plant trees by the roadsides and protect them so that they are not eaten by stray cattle. They should water them and see that they grow properly. Then we will have shade in summer and also fruits to eat. I think they should plant mango trees, don't you?' She knew my weakness for mangoes.

'Yes, but no one has asked us for our votes as yet,' I thought aloud.

We sat on the verandah with the papers, having small talk and thus spent our morning. We had lunch and sat down again waiting for someone to come. My wife began to yawn. After lunch she was used to a brief siesta. We sat waiting. And then our servants came out after finishing their chores and asked for permission to go out and cast their votes. The cook and the bearer, the maid and the gardener, the peon and the watchman, they were all there.

'Who are you going to vote for?' I asked them. One mentioned one party, the other another. Each one knew who he was going to vote for and for which party.

One by one they left. Some more time passed. My wife had already retired for her nap. I sat alone, my mind vacant. Suddenly on an impulse I got up. I must go to the office and check my mail, I said to myself.

When I came out in the street, I thought it was busier than ever. Several rickshaws were standing in a cluster. Nearby I espied our bearer. Beside him was his wife. The maid and her husband were also there. The gardener was there with his two wives. The driver's brother and his wife, the peon and his wife, the watchman with his aged parents and three young sisters, they were all there.

On one side of the group was one candidate's agent and on the other another candidate's agent, each one trying to drag them. And there were all those rickshaws to take this multitude to a booth hardly three hundred yards away.

And then I spotted the third candidate in person, with his folded hands, his face shining with perspiration, pleading and entreating in all humility a group of people standing before him! 'I have come myself, walking, just for you. Please vote for me. I am here in person to beg of you. You are the masters, sir, you are my masters…'

Master! With my single vote in my pocket on my way to the office, the word 'masters' kept ringing in my ears. And then the picture of our village of long ago flashed across my mind's eye. The zamindars, the high-born ones, whom we used to call 'the masters'. Their cattle could graze in any field. They could ask anyone in the street to do anything for them and it had to be done. Their wicked eye could fall on any young girl of the village with evil intent and none dared protest. They in their white clothes, as white as the cream in the milk which they drank. And then the prince and the princess, our neighbours in Amritsar. Their stories of princely grandeur and the secrets of the boudoir. And the little master, their son. 'For you are the masters, the real masters. I have come myself walking to seek your votes...' The words of the man in white khadi with folded hands continued to echo and re-echo in my ears ever so long as I walked away.

A Room '10 x '8

"**T**his room might be '10 x '8," said Mrs Malik pointing to a square in the draft plan lying on the table before them. It was the third time that she had made this suggestion. It seemed it didn't register on either her husband or the architect engaged to design the house.

The Maliks were going to have a house of their own in Delhi. They had purchased a plot in the most fashionable colony of the town sometime ago. Now that they were posted back in Delhi, they thought, they might as well have the house built.

In her heart of hearts Mrs Malik also

decided that after completion of the house, she would stay back in Delhi even if her husband was transferred to another station. She was sick of their postings. Every other year they were moved to a new place. Now that the children were grown-up, it was not desirable to shift them from school to school. Mrs Malik said, if he must, Mr Malik could go all alone. She would settle down permanently in Delhi with the children. She would have her mother-in-law for company. Mr Malik had no objection to it.

"This room might be '10 x '8," Mrs Malik repeated. Her husband was attending to a telephone call in the adjacent room.

"But this is a store." The architect explained to Mrs Malik.

"Yes, but I thought it could be my mother-in-law's room and after her it might be used as a storeroom."

The architect didn't seem to understand. He looked puzzled by Mrs Malik's observation.

"I mean... my mother-in-law could use the room for the present... As you know she is old and infirm... She isn't going to be there for...

and after her it could be converted into a storeroom." Mrs Malik explained haltingly.

Mr Malik joined them. Its seems while talking on the telephone he had also given thought to the suggestion. He too, was of the opinion that the store should be a little bigger. It is always better to have a commodious storeroom so that one can move about the trunks more freely. Then it is also more convenient to keep it tidy.

It was decided that the room adjacent to the kitchen should be '10 x '8. The courtyard would be a little narrower but that didn't matter much.

All the rest had already been provided and the plan was submitted for approval to the Corporation. Mrs Malik took an untiring interest in the construction of the house. She would be seen standing at the site with her umbrella throughout the day. She supervised every detail. At times she would give a hand to the masons and others. She was the first to arrive at the construction site and left after everyone had gone away. She ensured that there was no wastage of material and the labour did not idle about. Before long the house was completed. Mrs Malik insisted that she would have new furniture made for house; she would not let the old furniture enter the new house, not a piece of it.

They were still in the midst of plans to shift when they learnt that the house had been acquired by the Government. Mrs Malik was furious. But the next moment when Mr Malik mentioned the rent assessed, she quietened down.

While supervising the construction of the house, she had cultivated her neighbours; made friends in the colony. She thought of various plans for doing up the house. Everything had to be forgotten.

Then they were transferred from Delhi. Mrs Malik was happy. She would no more see her house, regret not being able to live in it and then thinking of the substantial rent, feel consoled. Transferred from one place to another, they had to wait for many more years for another term of posting in Delhi. In the meanwhile Mrs Malik's mother-in-law passed away. Their daughter had been married. In a way they were lucky that their house had been rented to the Government. Private tenants are such a headache. There is no end to their complaints and demands. And, then they are more often than not irregular in the payment of rent. Mrs Malik's house having been requisitioned by the Government, the rent was credited to their bank account every month regularly.

Only their son remained to be married now. Mr Malik thought that they would rather be done with it before he retired.

Their son had been married, Mr Malik had retired from service, but their house had not yet been released by the Government. Mr and Mrs Malik lived with their son and daughter-in-law in a rented house.

Mr Malik was still fighting with the Government for the release of the house when his end came. He passed away without being able to live in his house even for a day.

Now within three months the house was derequisitioned.

Mrs Malik's daughter-in-law was keener than Mrs Malik to shift to her own house. The moment they were restored possession of the house, she had it painted and polished and started shifting. The furniture dealer had been ordered to supply a number of pieces which he did.

They had to shift on Monday morning but as they woke up, they found that it was raining. The downpour was rather heavy. They waited and waited. Then it was time for Mrs Malik's son to go to the office. It was decided that they would shift in the evening.

It continued to rain throughout the day. It was raining as heavily as ever in the evening also. Monday being an auspicious day, Mrs Malik wanted to shift if they could. Tuesday was unthinkable; it was inauspicious.

Out of consideration for his mother the son decided to shift even though it continued to rain heavily. They sent for a taxi in addition to their own car and made a formal move. The rest of the luggage could be shifted later.

It was raining incessantly. Sitting in the back seat of the car, Mrs Malik was lost in memories.

What pains had she taken while the house was under construction! The days when she missed her meals! The days she stood in the scorching heat of the sun supervising the work in progress! The days she was drenched in rain!

The architect had prepared a sketch of the house in colour, the way it would look when completed. It had the figure of the lady of the house standing on the verandah with her back towards the marble pillar. Elegant and graceful. An image of contentment. Clad in a maroon saree. Mrs Malik felt that the architect had painted her. But she never wore maroon-coloured sarees. The figure in the sketch, however, was as tall as Mrs Malik. Reclining against the pillar she stood the way Mrs Malik used to stand. Mrs Malik saw the figure in the sketch and would go and stand before the dressing-table many a time. She thought that she must show that sketch to her daughter-in-law sometime.

Her daughter-in-law was sitting on the front seat with her husband. Moving the rear-view glass of the car towards her, she started repainting her lips. Where was the need to paint the lips when they were going to their own house? At the most they would eat and then go to sleep. Strange are the ways of modern girls! And how the girl talked! She was jabbering incessantly. Why must she talk with her own husband in English?

Mrs Malik had not picked up English. She had failed in this only. She had accomplished everything else in life. She drank. It becomes difficult always to refuse an offer of drink in the club. She learnt ballroom dancing. She danced with her own husband and with other's husbands also.

Suddenly it occurred to Mrs Malik that maybe the figure painted by the architect was that of her daughter-in-law. How could that be? She was nowhere on the scene when the plan of the house was prepared. But then, she was wearing a maroon-coloured saree that the figure in the sketch had. Yes, it was maroon colour. Mrs Malik never liked maroon colour. It was too loud for her taste. It was girls like her daughter-in-law who were fond of maroon colour.

"She can wear maroon, surely," said Mrs Malik to herself, "I wish she could also work as hard as I did. I had every brick of the house laid before my eyes. In sun and rain. I stood on the site supervising the construction from early in the morning till late in the night. Many a time I helped the masons with mortar and bricks. Many times I hauled the rubber pipe and sprayed water on the plastered wall."

Then they reached the house. His son drove the car straight to the porch and her daughter-in-law jumped out of it and there she stood reclining against the marble pillar on the verandah. Exactly the way the architect had painted the figure in the sketch. Mrs Malik felt a wrench in her heart. Maybe the architect had mocked at her.

Standing on the verandah, close to the pillar, trying to cover her elaborate hairdo with the maroon-coloured saree, her daughter-in-law was giving instructions to the servants about the luggage in the taxi following the car.

The luggage had been removed from the taxi. The taxi driver drove away after having been paid. Mrs Malik was still sitting on the back seat of their car. She had a strange sinking sensation.

Then her son and daughter-in-law entered the house. They put on the lights one by one. Every room was lit up. Mrs Malik looked on wide-eyed, still sitting in the back seat of her car. In the excitement nobody seemed to have remembered to open the door for her the way it was always done.

Suddenly her son thought of his mother. He ran to the porch and opened the door of the car.

"A drive in the evening always makes me go to sleep," the mother spoke in a whisper. Her daughter-in-law had also come out. Everyone was laughing. Mrs Malik's daughter-in-law was standing against the marble pillar on the verandah again. She was trying to cover her hairdo with her maroon-coloured saree.

"I am not going to eat. I have no appetite," said Mrs Malik, "I would like to sleep." The servants had laid dinner on the table.

"Then you better retire to your room," said the daughter-in-law pointing to room '10 x '8 and her son conducted Mrs Malik to it, holding her hand. She was feeling terribly drowsy.

"I thought it could be my mother-in-law's room and after her it might be converted into a store." Lying down on her bed, these words echoed in Mrs Malik's ears.

Mrs Malik shook her head again. But what was wrong with it? Her husband had already gone. She would follow him. One day she must do it.

"I thought it could be my mother-in-law's room and after her it might be converted into a store." The words re-echoed in Mrs Malik's ears.

And then she heard her daughter-in-law comment. "The house is otherwise very well planned. It lacks only a storeroom. I would like to have a big enough store."

Mrs Malik heard it and she felt as if she was sinking deep and deep into bottomless well.